T0368647

The Gardener and His Apple Tree

Written by Kyle Mireles

Illustrated by Katelyn Franke

AuthorHouse™
1663 Liberty Drive
Bloomington, IN 47403
www.authorhouse.com
Phone: 833-262-8899

This book is printed on acid-free paper.

ISBN: 979-8-8230-3677-1 (sc)
ISBN: 979-8-8230-3678-8 (e)

Library of Congress Control Number: 2024922639

Print information available on the last page.

Published by AuthorHouse 10/30/2024

author HOUSE®

Dedicated to the Lord Jesus Christ who gave Himself for sinners. May all honor, glory, power, dominion, and blessing be unto you forevermore Lord.
As well as to every Father and Mother in the Lord. May you have all wisdom, long-suffering, and grace to train your children in the way they should go. That they would bear fruit unto righteousness to the Glory of our God. Amen

There was a Gardener
who bought himself an Apple Tree.
He loved his Apple Tree very much.
But the Apple Tree was unaware
that its purpose was to produce
fruit.

Matthew 5:16

The Apple Tree
did not understand
the ways of the Gardener.
It was unsure if it
could trust the
Gardener.

1 Peter 2:2

5

With lots of sun, water,
and the Gardener, the Apple Tree's
roots began to grow deep.
But then it came time for pruning.
The Apple Tree was scared
when the Gardener pulled out a
pair of pruners.

John 15:2   Jeremiah 29:11

What are you going to do with those!?
I am going to cut back some of your branches, so that you grow up to be strong, and be able to bear the weight of the fruit you will produce.
W-w-w-why would you do that!? You're going to kill me!
I promise you that I will not harm you.

With a snip here and
a clip there, the Gardener
began to prune his Apple Tree.
Every move that he made was
gentle and with purpose. But even
though he made every cut perfect,
the Apple Tree now
felt exposed.

Gee Gardener,
why did you have to take off
so much? And why that branch?
That was a good branch.

"You see those little spots
at the top of the branches?"
"Yes Gardener, I do."
"I noticed those before I purchased you.
If they were to be left alone,
those spots would spread
and be your ruin."

"I see!
You really do care about me.
But Gardener, can I ask you something?
If I had black spots all over me,
then why did you purchase me?
I'm sure you could have found a much
better apple tree than me."

Romans 6:23

"The truth is Apple Tree,
that you, as well as all
the other trees, were brown,
brittle, and dead.
But I gave you life,
and I make all things new!"

Romans 6:23

I believe you Gardener. Thank you for picking me!
Please, if there is any way, go back for all the other trees;
so that they can have life and feel your love,
and be made new as well!

18

As the weeks
turned into months,
and the months turned into years,
Apple Tree grew and grew
under the loving care
of the Gardener.

Other trees were added to
the Gardener's orchard.
Every one receiving the same love,
and growing with the same purpose.
All because the Gardener was willing to
pay a great price
for each one!

1 Peter 1:18-19

The End

We come to Christ to save our own skin.
But changing hearts, we now look to Him.
No more thinking of our own.
But in ways that we can make His gospel known.
We might be scared, anxious, or of a feeble mind,
But all of this we leave behind.
For the only gospel worth sharing, boldly in the Lord thus declaring.
Not for our sakes, for we could die.
But for Him, our Lord who was lifted high.
We do not fear what men think or what they could do.
Because worth sharing is the love that saved both me and you.
Now we have something to believe in. And through this faith we bring all to Him.
No more thinking of our own, but the love that God Himself has shown.
Reconciling us to Himself on the cross, everything else in life is at a loss.
For Christ to be in us and us in Him,
We will work from the inside out, not the outside in.

By Kyle Mireles

Printed in the United States
by Baker & Taylor Publisher Services